Dear Parents,

Welcome to the Scholastic Reader series. We have taken more than 80 years of experience with teachers, parents, and children and put it into a program that is designed to match your child's interests and skills.

Level 1—Short sentences and stories made up of words kids can sound out using their phonics skills, and words that are important to remember.

Level 2—Longer sentences and stories with words kids need to know, and new "big" words that they will want to know.

Level 3—From sentences to paragraphs to longer stories, these books have large "chunks" of text and are made up of a rich vocabulary.

Level 4—First chapter books with more words and fewer pictures.

It is important that children learn to read well enough to succeed in school and beyond. Here are ideas for reading this book with your child:

- Look at the book together. Encourage your child to read the title and make a prediction about the story.
- Read the book together. Encourage your child to sound out words when appropriate. When your child struggles, you can help by providing the word.
- Encourage your child to retell the story. This is a great way to check for comprehension.
- Have your child take the fluency test on the last page to check progress.

Scholastic Readers are designed to support your child's efforts to learn how to read at every age and every stage. Enjoy helping your child learn to read and love to read.

　　　—Francie Alexander
　　　Chief Education Officer
　　　Scholastic Education

ISBN 0-439-87149-2

12 11 10 9 8 7 6 5 4 3 2 1   6 7 8 9 10 11/0

Printed in the U.S.A.
First printing, September 2006

I LIKE MYSELF!

by Hans Wilhelm

Scholastic Reader — Level 1

SCHOLASTIC INC.

New York   Toronto   London   Auckland   Sydney
Mexico City   New Delhi   Hong Kong   Buenos Aires

There are my friends.
They are going to play
in the park.

Wait for me!
I love Frisbee.

I want to play, too.

Please let me catch
the Frisbee!

I missed.

Oh, no.
I missed again.

I hate this game.
It's no fun.

I am just too small.
I can't do anything right.

I am not as good
as the others.

Wait!
That's not true!

Hi, guys.
Need some help?

I got it!

I can do things that
others can't do.

Some of us are tall,
and some of us are small.

I like myself
just the way I am.